# Moby Dick

# The Young Collector's
# Illustrated Classics

# Moby Dick

By
Herman Melville

Adapted by
Donna Carlson

# Contents

Chapter 1
Leaving the Land. . . . . . . . . . . . . . . .9

Chapter 2
The *Pequod*. . . . . . . . . . . . . . . .27

Chapter 3
Captain Ahab. . . . . . . . . . . . . . . .45

Chapter 4
Sighting a Whale. . . . . . . . . . . . .59

Chapter 5
Stubb Kills a Whale. . . . . . . . . . . .79

Chapter 6
The *Jungfrau*. . . . . . . . . . . . . . .97

Chapter 7
    Moby Dick. . . . . . . . . . . . . . . . . . . .109

Chapter 8
    A Battle. . . . . . . . . . . . . . . . . . . .127

Chapter 9
    Chasing the Whale. . . . . . . . . . . .141

Chapter 10
    Disaster. . . . . . . . . . . . . . . . . . .153

Chapter 11
    The Rescue. . . . . . . . . . . . . . . . . .175

# Chapter

1

# Leaving The Land

My name is Ishmael. Some years ago, having no money in my pocket, I went to sea. I thought that I would sail around and see the watery part of the world.

Even now, whenever I feel as if it is a damp, drizzly November day inside of me, I think that it is high time to get to sea as soon as I can. I long to be out there at the horizon—that place on the water where the sea seems to meet the sky. It is where people on land lose sight of the sea. But the world does not end at the horizon. For me, the horizon is where the world begins.

One morning I awoke with this rest-

less feeling and went out for a walk. I found myself wandering down to the sea. I sat on the dock and dreamily stared out over the ocean. How I love to stand on the deck and feel the warmth of the sun on my back and the cool spray of a salty breeze tingle my cheek and ruffle my hair. The best way to go to sea is as a sailor— with water all around and a huge blue sky above.

Sitting there, I looked at the boats that were tied to the dock. The waves gently rocked the boats from side to side, causing them to creak and groan, as if they were restless to get back to the sea. It was then I decided to leave the land and return to the sea.

Feeling free and happy, I returned to my room and stuffed a shirt or two into my old suitcase. There was no time to lose now. I had made up my mind.

Soon I was on my way. When I reached New Bedford it was already dark, and I found I had missed the last boat to Nantucket.

I was hungry and tired, so I looked for a place to eat and sleep. As I had only a few pieces of silver, I had to choose a place that was not too expensive.

After searching awhile, I came upon a place called *The Spouter Inn*. It looked dark and shabby. But, being so tired, I was glad to find any place that offered something to eat and a bed to sleep in.

"It is probably cheap," I thought to

myself. "I may as well go in and see if there's a place for me."

As I pushed the door open I noticed the walls were covered with rusty old spears, called harpoons, used to kill whales. Next to these were huge, old whale teeth that gleamed in the dim light.

I crossed the room to where a group of sailors were sitting at a table, carving figures out of the bones and teeth of whales. I watched awhile before asking for the landlord.

When he arrived I was disappointed

to hear him say, "Well now, lad. The inn is all full."

Seeing my sad face he said, "How about your sharing a bed with a harpooner? Looks to me like you're going whalin', so you'd better get used to that sort of thing."

The thought of going back out into the cold night air to search again for a place to sleep was more than I could bear. So I accepted his offer.

I sat down heavily on a wooden stool and watched the men carve their scrimshaw.

Finally, we were called to supper. It was wonderful to see the hearty meal of beef, potatoes, and dumplings. When I finished, I sat back to rest. Suddenly my eyes began to feel very heavy. So, I was glad when the landlord showed me to my room.

"When will the harpooner come to bed?" I asked.

"Oh, you never know with that one, lad. He sometimes stays out late trying to

sell the shrunken heads he collects on his sailing voyages. Just go to sleep. He'll be back soon."

Although I was very tired, I had trouble falling asleep. I found myself glancing

around the room, wondering when the harpooner would come. I dozed for awhile, then my eyes shot open as I heard some-one at the door. A huge figure entered, carrying a candle.

The candlelight shone on his face—such a face! It was a dark purplish-yellow color, covered here and there with dark squares. When he took off his hat I saw that he had no hair on his shiny purplish head except for one twisted knot on the top. It looked like the scalp-knot on the shrunken heads he sold.

I was very frightened at the sight of him. Trembling under the covers, I wanted to run, but was so scared I could not move. But he did not look at me and began to undress. To my horror I saw that his arms, legs, and chest were covered with these same dark square tattoos.

Then, he did something very strange. He fumbled in his pocket and took out a small, ugly doll with a hunched back. He set it in the fireplace, lit a match, and started a little fire in front of it. I realized that this object was a wooden idol.

He knelt down in front of the doll, began to sway back and forth, and to sing a weird song. Was he praying? Maybe this man was the devil! I became more afraid.

He then got up, put out the fire, and returned the idol to his pocket. Suddenly he jumped into bed beside me. I screamed in terror.

"Who you?" he yelled in surprise.

I was so frozen with fear, I could not answer him.

"Speakee to me!" he said.

I saw him grab his tomahawk, but still I could not move. As he came toward me, I somehow managed a scream, and then I yelled out, "Save me!"

Footsteps were coming toward the door from outside. Then, the landlord rushed in. He took one look at both me and Queequeg, and then he laughed. "Don't be afraid, lad," he said. "Queequeg here wouldn't harm a hair on your head."

"But he's a cannibal!" I screamed. "He prays to an idol and has tattoos from head to toe!"

The landlord put his hand on my shoulder.

"No need to worry," he said. "He has his ideas and we have ours. He may be strange, but he would not hurt anyone. I am sure of that."

I looked over at Queequeg. In the light of the lamp he still looked odd, but not mean. I realized that Queequeg had been as frightened of me as I was of him, since he had not known that I was in the bed.

"Queequeg," said the landlord. "This

man sleepee with you. You sabbee, Queequeg?"

"Me sabbee," he said with a friendly grin.

He motioned with his big hand for me to get into the bed. He seemed friendly

enough, so I wasn't so afraid as before. I got in the bed and pulled up the covers, very tired and glad to rest.

I did ask this strange man to take the tomahawk out of the bed and leave it on the other side of the room. He seemed to understand that it bothered me. He removed it from the bed quickly.

He then climbed into his side of the bed and blew out the candle. Soon I heard his long, slow snores. This did not bother me. It was as gentle and soothing as a lullaby.

I lay there in the dark for awhile, thinking about the events of the day. It had been a long, tiring journey to New Bedford.

I thought about the sailors downstairs who talked of the sea as they carved their scrimshaw. They had sat hunched over the table, leaning towards the lamp lit with whale oil. Their knives chipped away at the hard, white ivory, sending little bits skittering in all directions.

One or two of them were expert at the

craft, and as they whittled I could see the shapes beginning to form on their pieces of bone—a ship in full sail or a sea gull.

Then, I thought of Queequeg. I smiled a little remembering my terror at first seeing him. I had never in my life seen such a strange-looking man. But now, when I looked over at him sleeping so soundly, I had a good, safe feeling.

As I began to fall asleep, I thought to myself that you cannot always tell what the inside of a person is like by just looking at the outside.

I never slept better in my life.

# Chapter

## 2

# The Pequod

Early the next day, all the sailors sat down together for breakfast. Their faces had the look of men who live outdoors. Tanned brown as coconuts, the older ones had faces as hard as leather and cracked from squinting into the sun.

Queequeg sat at the head of the table. He was quiet and cool as an icicle. Reaching his arm over to the middle of the table, he speared a steak with the tip of a harpoon. He did not eat any of the rolls and coffee but just kept gobbling the beefsteaks. When he finished, he left the table to sit in the corner and smoke his pipe.

It was a lovely morning, and I decided

to go out for a walk. Shops lined the winding streets that sloped down to the sea. I walked along the water's edge and stopped to look at the great ships. I dreamed of my voyage to come.

When I returned to *The Spouter Inn*, I saw Queequeg smoking his pipe by the fire and sitting with a big book in his lap. He was only looking at the pictures. I realized he could not read.

I went over and offered to read to him, and he accepted. He was very happy as I read the story. He often made a noise of approval, and he even laughed out loud. I began to laugh with him, and I found that he was a good companion.

After reading to him awhile, we started talking, and this is when our friendship began. I asked him how he came to be in New Bedford with all the sailors.

In short words and poor English, Queequeg told me the story. He said he was a native of Kokovoko, a faraway island in the South Pacific. His father was a high-chief. Queequeg lived a good life

there, but he had a strong desire to see more of the world.

One day, a foreign ship stopped to visit his father's island. Queequeg paddled his canoe out to the ship, climbed the

rope ladder, and hid on deck. The next day, already far out to sea, he was discovered. At first the captain was angry, but Queequeg soon proved to be a strong seaman and a skillful harpooner.

Queequeg explained to me that his world was very different from ours. However, one thing he learned quickly, he said, was that within all groups of people there are kind men and there are unkind men.

I told Queequeg my own life story. Then I told him of my desire to go whale hunting, and he offered to teach me. I accepted, shaking his hand excitedly.

We planned to start out the next day for Nantucket, where we could find a whaling ship and begin our adventure.

We talked about whaling until the landlord called us to supper. After finish-

ing our meal, we went to bed. We had to awake at dawn to catch the boat to Nantucket.

We arrived the next day on Nantucket Island. Surrounded by water, the people there are connected to the sea from the time they learn to walk. With the sand beneath their feet, they breathe the salt air and fling their poles into the water for fish. Their lives depend on the sea, and many men from Nantucket become some of the world's finest whaling seamen.

We made our way along the beach, stopping to ask if anyone knew of a whaling ship that needed help. We learned there was a ship named the *Pequod* about to leave on a long voyage. Arriving at the ship, we saw on deck a tall man dressed in a blue coat, scowling down at us.

"Ahoy!" I cried to him. "Are you the captain of this ship?"

"Why do you want to know?" he called back, still frowning.

"We want to join up with you," I said.

"I'm not the captain. I'm the owner of

this ship. Peleg's the name. Know anything about whaling?" he asked.

"No, sir. But I want to learn. And my friend here will help me," I replied.

"Oh, is your friend there such a great harpooner, then?" asked Peleg.

Before I could answer, Queequeg stepped towards the man and said, "You see dat spot of tar on beach far away?"

"Yes, I see it," said Peleg, looking far off onto the deserted beach.

Queequeg picked up his harpoon, and with a great heave of his arm, the harpoon sailed through the air and landed

exactly on the spot of tar! He then looked over at Peleg and said coolly, "If dat spot was a whale, dat whale be dead."

Peleg had been around ships all his life. He had sailed the seas with some of the best seamen in the world, but even he was surprised at Queequeg's skill.

"Sign on, men!" he yelled to us.

We ran up on deck, and Peleg took out some papers for us to sign. I scrawled my name across the bottom of the page. Queequeg, who could not write, dipped the pen into the ink. Quickly and neatly, he made his mark on the page. It looked like this — ✠ . I noticed that it was the same mark as a tattoo on his arm.

This done, I said to Peleg, "When do we meet the captain, sir?"

He frowned. "No worry, lad. That's none of your concern. Captain Ahab is not feeling very well these days, but he'll be fine once the voyage is under way."

I had a feeling that something was wrong, but I tried to put it out of my mind. We left the ship and began walking away from the water when a stranger pulled on my jacket and stopped us.

"Mates, have you signed with the *Pequod?*" he asked us.

He was a strange and shabby man, dressed in a faded jacket and patched

trousers. A rag of a black handkerchief was tied about his neck. He pointed a dirty finger in my face.

He asked again, "Have you signed with that ship?"

"Yes, we have," I said. I started to go.

"Have you seen 'Old Thunder' yet?"

"Who is 'Old Thunder'?" I asked him.

"Captain Ahab," he answered.

"Why do you call him 'Old Thunder'?"

"Because when he gives an order he roars like thunder in a storm," he replied. "Did you hear about his leg?"

"No. What of it?" I said.

"He lost it to a whale. Now he has a leg carved from a whale's jawbone," said the stranger.

My stomach gave a little kick when he said this. He put his scraggly face up close to mine and whispered, "There's to be strange troubles on that ship, mates. Yes sir. Well, good day to you." Then he was gone.

I remembered the uneasy feeling I had earlier that day. But again I tried to forget it. It was a fine day, and Queequeg and I wanted to celebrate joining the crew of the *Pequod*.

Queequeg and I began to talk of other things.

# Chapter

3

# Captain Ahab

The next few days were spent in busy preparation for the voyage. The old sails needed mending, and new sails were being brought aboard. Harpoons, food, water, and fuel were also being loaded.

The sailors raced around trying to complete preparation for the journey. I was learning my way around the ship and getting very excited about my whaling adventure.

At last, when everything was ready, and the orders were given to sail, I felt a chill run up my spine. Then I heard the order, "Man the vessel! Blood and thunder! Drive 'em aft!" My dream of becoming a

whaler had come true. We were on our
way!

For several days after leaving
Nantucket, nothing was seen of Captain
Ahab. I was curious to see this man with
one leg who roared like thunder, but I was
a bit frightened, too. Meanwhile, I met the
rest of the crew.

There were three chief officers on board. Starbuck was the first mate. He was a native of Nantucket and knew the sea as well as he knew his name. Stubb was the second mate. He was a fun-loving fellow who puffed on his pipe all day. The third mate was Flask. He was short and stocky, but a good sailor all the same.

Queequeg, of course, was a harpooner. There were two other harpooners on the ship as well—Tashtego and Daggoo. I

was one of dozens of sailors aboard. They were of all shapes and sizes and spoke many different languages.

From talking with the crew, I learned about the importance of whaling. Cities all around the world depended on whaling for money and jobs. Many people became rich from whaling. Some people who lived on the land did not like whalers. They did not like to see the whales killed, and they worried about the danger to the sailors.

Most of the sailors did not think about these things too much. Right or wrong, this was what they did. Whaling was an important part of their lives, and they didn't know how to do anything else.

One misty morning, I stood on deck and watched the dark waters churning below, tossing the ship recklessly. The waves sprayed icy foam high into the air, and tiny chinks of ice dashed against my face and chest.

Through the fog I could see the figure of a man. As the mist cleared a little, I noticed he had only one leg!

# Moby Dick

He did not speak a word, but stood there looking straight out over the water. As I watched him, a shiver ran over me.

Days passed, and we glided far out to sea. At night the sky was like an immense black velvet tent, glittering with a million twinkling jewels. The days were blue and breezy.

One clear day, a group of us were on deck doing our chores, when a whisper swiftly passed through the men, "Captain Ahab is on deck!" We looked up and there he stood, silently waiting for the men to gather around. Every man dropped what he was doing and came forward.

For several moments he did not say a word. Then suddenly he shouted, "What do you do when you see a whale, men?"

"Sing out to the sailors!" their voices cried.

"And what do you do next, men?"

"Lower the boats, and go after him!" the men shouted.

Ahab motioned to the sailors to gather around close.

"Listen here and listen well! Keep your eyes open and look sharp. Look out for a great white whale!"

Tashtego spoke out. "Captain Ahab, is this the great white whale that is called Moby Dick?"

"Aye!" cried Ahab. "That's the one! Do you know him?"

Some of the crew said they knew the whale. They had seen him on other voyages.

"Was that the whale that took your leg, captain?" asked Starbuck.

"Aye, the very one!" answered Ahab, with fury in his eyes. "He got hold of my leg and bit it right off at the knee. Left me forever to walk with a stump."

Ahab shook his fist at the sky and shouted, "Aye, but I will get that whale! I will chase him round the world! Are you with me men?"

"Aye, aye!" shouted the harpooners.

"God bless you," Ahab half-shouted, half-sobbed. He took out of his pocket a solid gold coin and hammered it to the masthead.

"Whoever spots him first will earn this gold piece."

The sailors cheered and shouted.

Ahab looked to his first mate and saw that Starbuck stood away from the others and did not join in their cheers.

"Mr. Starbuck, why the long face? Will

you not chase the white whale? Are you not brave enough for Moby Dick? This would surprise me."

Starbuck stepped forward.

"I am brave enough for any whale, captain," he said. "I have seen the beast with its crooked jaw and huge spout that spits fury. I know my work. It is not Moby Dick I fear."

"What then, Starbuck? Speak out."

"It is *you* I fear, Captain Ahab. Your anger at the whale is too great; your fury places us in danger. I came on this voyage to hunt whales—any whale. You are here to kill Moby Dick. You want the whale that took your leg. Your anger asks for more than bravery. It asks for our lives."

Ahab listened to Starbuck, but seemed not to hear his words. He looked to his crew and shouted out for all to hear, "Are you not one and all with Ahab, your captain? This is to be a great hunt! You men were born to kill this whale, this greatest of all beasts. It is to be the grandest adventure of your lives and mine!"

Captain Ahab ordered mugs of rum for everyone. Lifting his goblet high into the air, his voice rang out, "Drink, you harpooners! Drink, you seamen! Drink to the death of Moby Dick!"

The men raised their mugs.

"Death to Moby Dick!" they all cried.

Starbuck took a sip too, but a shadow fell over his face.

# Chapter

4

# Sighting A Whale

Life at sea was hard work. I was learning something new about whaling everyday.

We were hunting the whales to get the rich oil from their fat, or blubber. The blubber was boiled in big pots until it melted into oil. This oil was used around the world for lamps. Whale oil burned clean, without smoke, and for a long time. When the oil hardened, it turned to wax, which was used to make candles. Lamps and candles were the only way people had to light their homes at night. That is why whaling was so important.

Many weeks went by, and we had not

yet seen a whale. One day the sea was very calm, and the men were sitting out on the deck weaving rugs they made from straw-like rope. Tashtego was sitting high up in the masthead keeping a lookout. The men were singing and whistling sea songs.

Suddenly from above, Tashtego cried out, "There she blows!" He had spotted a whale! Everyone dropped his weaving and stood up to look where Tashtego was pointing.

My heart was pounding as I pushed through the men to get a better look.

"At last," I said to myself. This was the moment I had been waiting for!

Off in the distance, a thin stream of bubbles shooting straight up in the air could be seen. Then another. And another. It was a whole group of whales.

There are many kinds and sizes of whales. They are not really fish; they are mammals. Fish breathe through their gills underwater, but whales must swim to the surface for air. They breathe through a hole on the top of their head called a spout, and they blow out a shower of mist like a water fountain. When a sailor sees this burst of spray, he knows it is a whale.

My hands trembled with excitement. My mind was spinning, trying to remember what I was supposed to do.

Suddenly Captain Ahab appeared on deck. He yelled out to all the sailors, "All hands on deck! Get the boats in the water."

The crew was running in all directions. One boat was already in the water, and the men were holding their oars.

Ahab reached down to lift the deck hatch, and five strange yellow-skinned

men scrambled out. Ahab did not seem at all surprised to see these men.

"Who are they?" I asked.

"Stowaways," said Stubb.

Captain Ahab had brought them aboard to help with the hunt. These men were from Manilla, where whale hunters were said to be the most fearless in the world.

The captain turned to the rest of his crew and gave the order, "Lower away!

What are you waiting for, you dogs? After the whale!"

To the strange men from Manilla he gave additional orders. Then he turned to

me and the other men staring at the stow-aways. "What are you doing standing there staring? Get going, men!"

We all knew what to do. The other whaling boats, hung by ropes along the sides of the great ship, were lowered into

the water. We jumped into the boats to set off to catch up with the whale. A few other sailors remained on board, pulling hard on the heavy ropes that lowered our boats down into the sea.

Once the boats hit the water, the men still on deck took great leaps off the *Pequod* and landed in the whaling boats.

"To the whales, men!" shouted Ahab.

Taking hold of the oars, the crew bent way over until their noses touched their knees. Then they pulled the oars hard through the water, their heads coming up all together in one motion like a wave. They did this again and again as Captain Ahab shouted at them, "Pull harder, lads! Break your backs! Faster to the whale!"

I was sitting toward the middle of one of the boats, rowing as fast and hard as I could. Every muscle in my body worked, tugging at the oars as the boats streamed swiftly over the water. My face and neck were drenched in sweat.

"After the whale!" cried Ahab.

We kept rowing and rowing, and I

thought my back would break from the pain of stretching so hard. My fingers stung from pulling on the rough wooden oars. The muscles in my arms and legs bulged hard as rocks under my skin.

"Why can't you pull harder, you sea dogs? Stop sleeping. We have a whale to kill! Get going!" screamed Ahab.

The boats climbed the waves, bows pointing up to the sky. Reaching the top of the wave, the boat dipped over the knife-like edge and sent us crashing downward again. Up and down. Up and down. Riding the sea was like a dangerous sleigh ride, the white foam waving and curling below.

We rowed close to the spot where the whales had been, but we could not see the spouts anymore. Not sure where to go, the men stopped rowing, and the boats gently bobbed up and down like corks in the rough sea. We could see nothing except the still surface of the blue water.

Ahab stood up and leaned on his ivory leg. He held his hand across his brow to keep the sun out of his eyes. He turned his head slowly from side to side. The school of whales must have gone down deep into the water.

"Every man look out for the whale," Ahab yelled. "Queequeg, stand up! Find the whale!"

Queequeg dropped his oar and jumped up. His huge purplish back twisted and turned as he carefully searched the sea.

In another boat Flask stood up to

look, but he was short and could not see very far. Daggoo, his harpooner, said, "Mr. Flask, I will lift you into the air, sir."

In one quick motion, Daggoo hoisted Flask up high onto his broad shoulders. Then a moment later, in a third boat, Tashtego shouted, "There they are!"

Some distance away there was greenish-white foam bubbling above the water's surface.

"Grab the oars, men," said Starbuck.

"Sing out and pull, lads!" shouted Flask.

"Burst your lungs, men!" screamed Stubb.

The chase was on. The water danced beneath the boats. Over the huge rolling waves we went. We were pulling with all our might, but the water was rough and choppy. It was very difficult to stay on course.

A foggy mist appeared out of nowhere. And then it curled around us so we could not see past the tip of the boat. We kept rowing, trying to get through the fog.

Just then we heard a sound I will never forget. It was a strange groan, deep and loud, coming from under the water. It sounded like distant thunder. But it was not. It was the sound of the whales below the surface of the sea.

The mist rolled away, and we saw the back of a gigantic whale surfacing not more than twenty feet away from us.

"There's his hump! Give it to him, Queequeg," whispered Starbuck.

Queequeg dropped his oar and grabbed his harpoon. He drew back his arm, taking a second to steady his aim. With one great motion he threw that spear straight at the whale. The harpoon sank deep into the whale's side.

The whale slid under the boat. He rolled like an earthquake beneath us. Then the boat shot out of the water high into the air, and the men tumbled out and crashed down into the sea.

The men choked on saltwater and gulped for air.

One minute I was flying through the air, and the next, I was plunging headfirst into the water, knocking the wind out of my lungs. For a moment I did not know what happened, but I quickly fanned my legs like a fish struggling to get to the surface.

The whale swam away. The men, gulping for air and choking on saltwater, grabbed at oars and the sides of the boat. All our strength gone, we weakly pulled ourselves up into the boat.

The water in the boat was almost up to our knees, and we had to bale it out. Then, we sat back for a minute and took deep breaths of air.

We looked around, but the other boats and the *Pequod* were not in sight. We called out into the emptiness, but no one answered.

Banged and bruised, we were greatly worried when we saw the sun going down. In a little while the boat was drifting in total darkness.

At last, Starbuck managed to strike the waterproof match to light our lantern, but no one saw our sign for help. Soaking wet and shivering cold, we bobbed through the long night. Our lamp gave off an eerie glow, guiding us into the black unknown that lay before us.

# Chapter

5

# Stubb Kills A Whale

After many hours, the sky began to whiten as morning arrived. Through the dewy mist a large shadow appeared, and we heard the faint creaking of ropes and slapping of water against wood. The *Pequod!*

We shouted and cried in joy as we straightened our oars and rowed towards the ship. She looked like a big mother hen waiting for her chicks to come back home to her.

Weary, but with tears of happiness, we hoisted our boats up to the topsides. Once aboard, we cruised the sea, searching for the other men.

By mid-morning we found the others, stranded and waiting for rescue. They were so tired they could barely speak. One by one, the men were dragged up on deck, all very sore and looking half-dead.

I will never forget the looks on their faces as they came on board the *Pequod*. We all fell over one another hugging for joy and relief. We were tired but very over-joyed. *We were alive!*

I looked over at Queequeg and asked him, "Does this happen very often?"

He put his big hand on my shoulder, looked down at me, and said, "Yes, Ishmael. This is the way it will be."

I shivered in my wet clothes and wondered to myself, "What other surprises does the sea have waiting for me?"

Captain Ahab was very quiet. Once he was sure all the men were safe on board, he did not join in our excited chatter as we gathered on deck to relive our adventure. He stood alone, away from the others, and looked out over the ocean, still searching for Moby Dick.

Many weeks passed without our seeing another whale. Then one quiet night
under a huge, silver-dollar moon, a sailor
cried down from the masthead.

"There she blows!"

Out in the distance, below the bright
stars, could be seen a fountain of bubbles
shining against the black sea.

Because it was night, there would be no whale hunt. The sailor had called out just to tell us that whales were in the area. I stared out at that spot of shiny bubbles and felt my stomach dip as I remembered what had happened the last time. Then I went to my bunk below to go to sleep. As my eyes closed, I wondered what adventures the next whale hunt would bring.

But the next day, the whales were not seen again. As if they knew someone or something was chasing them, they slipped away.

Again it was many weeks before we saw another whale. We sailed into the Indian Ocean, and the water was very calm.

One day it was my turn on top of the masthead. I enjoyed this duty because I liked to look out and watch the flying fish and dolphins playfully leap out of the water.

Occasionally, we would cruise near an island, and I wondered if the natives

were watching us with curiosity. I imagined them standing near the shore under the palm trees. Perhaps they had their spears in hand as they looked out at the great *Pequod*.

The sun was warm, and I began to feel drowsy when I was startled by a sudden burst of bubbles from the water. Close by was a huge sperm whale! It seemed to roll along, big as a boat. Its back was as shiny as a mirror.

Ahab spotted the whale when I did, and soon the whaling boats glided off quietly so we would not scare away the whale.

It must have seen us because suddenly it turned and flipped its huge tail forty feet in the air! Then it sank out of sight. For several moments the boat rocked from side to side, and we hung on for dear life.

After awhile the water calmed a bit, and we looked around us for the whale. Just when we thought it was gone, its huge head pushed out of the water, only a

# Moby Dick

few yards from Stubb's boat.

"Go get it men!" said Stubb. "Keep cool. Keep cool."

Forgetting their fear, the men rowed ahead until the whale and Stubb were face to face.

"Stand up, Tashtego! Come here and give it to him!"

Tashtego jumped up and sailed his harpoon straight into the whale. It was a perfect shot. The whale dove down into the water, causing huge waves that turned the boat around and around as if it were caught in a whirlpool.

"Turn the boat around!" yelled Stubb.

The oarsmen pulled hard on the oars, digging into the swirling sea to spin the boat around to face the whale. The giant head came up again. Its mouth opened wide, showing huge, pointed white teeth.

Stubb grabbed a spear and plunged it into the whale's mouth. Bright red blood poured out of its head. He speared it again and again.

The whale's body shook for some

time, and then all the life went out of it.

"He's dead, Mr. Stubb," said Daggoo.

"Yes. Haul him in, lads," said Stubb. A proud look shone on his face. He knew he had done his job well, and he grinned behind his pipe.

The excitement of the chase and the kill was over. Now began the long, slow job of pulling the enormous animal back to

the ship. Stubb's whale had been killed far from the ship. This made the work even harder.

The three boats circled around the whale as the men lifted the long, heavy coils of rope. These were tied to the harpoons that were sticking out of the whale like needles in a pincushion. Long lines of rope led from the whale to the boats, and when everything was ready, orders were given to go.

There were six men in each boat, eighteen in all. We all leaned over and took hold of the oars. At the same time, our thirty-six arms gave a great pull on the oars.

I thought my spine would snap from the weight of that whale! It is hard enough to row the boats through the water with-

out the whale, but with it the work is nearly impossible. With each pull, I thought my arm would break; my hands were rubbed raw from my tight grip on the oars.

The work was slow and exhausting. We were only able to go a few inches with each stroke. Darkness came. Finally, we saw the lanterns on the ship.

Captain Ahab had stayed on board. As we drew closer, we saw him standing on deck waiting for us. When he saw the boats, he lowered the lamps to light our way.

When all were back on board, Ahab stood there frowning. He had a strange look on his face. He knew the men had worked very hard and had all done a fine job, but we all knew that he was thinking of Moby Dick. That was the whale he had wanted! That was the whale that had taken his leg. He would not sleep in peace until Moby Dick was dead.

Ahab watched the crew struggle with the whale, and then he turned and went

to his cabin. As he walked away, his ivory peg gleamed brightly in the darkness under the moonlight.

We still had much work to do. Once the whale was snugly fastened to the ship, the men could rest from their day's work. Heavy iron chains were dragged along the deck. When pulled alongside the ship, the head of the whale hugged the bow, and its tail met the stern. Here the whale stayed all night, attached to the ship by the chains and ropes.

Sharks, smelling the scent of the whale, swam to the *Pequod* and nibbled on the meat. The sharks circled the ship and bit chunks of fat off the whale—only a few inches from where the sailors were sleeping inside the hold of the ship!

# Chapter

6

# The
# Jungfrau

In many parts of the world, whale meat is a common food. Eskimos eat whale meat everyday. Many years ago, it was thought of as a very special treat. Kings paid high prices to feast on whale. But sailors usually don't eat whale meat.

I had never tasted whale meat, and my stomach did not agree with the idea of eating such a creature. Most of the other whalers felt as I did. After such a long battle with the whale, we did not want to go back to the ship and eat it. But we did sometimes dip our biscuits into the huge oil-pots and let them fry there awhile. That tasted delicious!

The next morning we were all up very early to begin the long, slow task of cutting up the whale to melt the blubber for oil. I looked over the side of the ship and was surprised to see how much of the body had been eaten by the sharks.

Tashtego tied a knot of rope to the deck and climbed down to the head of the whale. A large, sharp knife and a heavy, iron bucket were then lowered down to him. He knew just where to make a cut in the whale's smooth forehead. He did it in one clean stroke.

The huge whale was eighty feet long. Its head alone measured about twenty-five feet. The head was so deep that a long rope was tied to a bucket and dropped down into the hole Tashtego had made in the head of the whale. When he pulled it up again, it was full of oil that looked like milk. The oil was pulled up on deck and poured into a big tub. Then the bucket was lowered again. This went on for some time.

Then a terrible thing happened.

Tashtego was about to lower the bucket again when he slid on the slippery surface of the whale's skin and fell headfirst into the whale's head!

The men watching above cried out in horror. Queequeg was the first to act.

Quick as a cat, he dropped to the whale and dived in. When he appeared again, he had his arm tightly around Tashtego's neck. The two men were covered in creamy, white whale oil.

Queequeg dragged Tashtego to safety and pumped the liquid from his lungs. It came up like spilled pearls. Tashtego was breathing normally again! I looked at Queequeg and thought to myself, what a fine, brave man he is!

But, of course, all whalers were brave. At one time, the greatest whalers in the world were Dutch and German. Now, they no longer were, but once in awhile we saw a Dutch or German flag on a passing ship. One day we met one of these ships, called the *Jungfrau.*

When ships pass, the men wave to one another or shout some piece of news. But usually there is no more contact than that. However, the *Jungfrau* seemed very eager to greet us.

The captain of the *Jungfrau* stood high in the bow waving his arms. He

# Moby Dick

called out for us to meet him, and Ahab called back to him. Then, we shifted our direction, and our two ships glided gently alongside one another.

The *Jungfrau* lowered a boat for the captain, named Derick, to cross over to the *Pequod*. While this was happening, the men gathered at the side rails of the ships to chat like neighbors over a fence.

Once Captain Derick was aboard the *Pequod*, Captain Ahab was there to greet him. Ahab wasted no time.

"Have you seen Moby Dick, the great white whale?" he asked.

"No," Captain Derick said, shaking his head. "I don't know that whale. I have come to borrow some oil. We have not yet caught a whale and have no oil to light our lanterns."

Captain Ahab looked very disappointed. "Where is that whale?" he muttered to himself.

Ahab gave orders for some oil barrels to be given to the *Jungfrau*. It seemed curious for a whaling ship to be borrowing oil on whale ground, yet such a thing did happen.

The barrels were lowered overboard to the *Jungfrau's* whaling boats. These were then carried to their ship. The men joked and talked of "spouters" and "blubber-boilers" as they passed across the barrels. This done, they waved good-bye and shouted cheerful farewells.

Just as the whaling boats were heading back to the *Jungfrau*, a school of eight whales pushed their humps out of the sea. They rushed through the water like a team of horses. Behind them was another whale, a huge, yellowish one. It looked

sickly, and from the size of its crusty, yellow hump it must have been very old.

Captain Derick was so excited at seeing the whales that he almost knocked the oil barrels into the water. Since he had not yet caught a whale, and since the oil he borrowed would not last very long, he wanted very badly to catch this whale. He jumped up and started shouting orders to his men, who were so surprised to finally see a whale, that for a short time there was much confusion aboard the *Jungfrau*.

The *Pequod's* crew laughed at the sight and gathered around to watch. The big, old whale emerged again and gave out a sickly groan.

"Maybe he has a stomachache," joked Stubb. "Think of it! A stomachache fifty feet long!"

As the whale surfaced higher we could see it had only one fin.

"Wait, old chap," said Flask to the whale, "I'll make you a sling for that stump."

Then Stubb yelled, "Who says it's the

*Jungfrau's* whale, men? I say it's *anybody's* whale. What do you say? Should we join the chase?"

Loud cheers went up from the crew.

"Aye. Aye."

"After the whale!"

"May the best man win!"

With great speed the men scrambled to let down the boats. Soon they were swiftly rowing towards the whale. The other eight whales, having sensed the danger, were well out of reach. It was the old, yellow whale that was being hunted now—one that would yield many barrels of oil.

The *Jungfrau's* boats were quite a bit ahead, leaving choppy waters for the *Pequod* crew. This angered Stubb, who cried, "Those ungrateful dogs! That's the thanks they give us for our oil! Are we going to let those rascals beat us?"

"No!" yelled the men.

"Then, after them, men! A bottle of brandy to the man who sinks the whale!" promised Stubb.

The chase was on, and the *Pequod* crew soon managed to overtake Captain Derick's boats. But once out in the wide waters, it was the whale who had out-smarted us all. We waited for over an hour, but the whale had escaped and was nowhere to be seen.

As the sun began to set, we turned our boats around and headed back to the ship. In the last light of day, we could see the sails of the *Jungfrau* in the distance continuing her search for whales.

# Chapter

7

# Moby Dick

It had been well over a month since our meeting with the *Jungfrau*, and everyone rushed on deck to see another fine ship coming our way. An English flag waved on high. It was the *Samuel Enderby*.

As the ship drew near, Ahab went to the rails. "Have you seen Moby Dick?" Ahab shouted, waving a harpoon over his head.

"Aye! Years ago. And he took my arm," yelled back their captain.

"And my leg!" called Ahab. "Have you seen him this voyage?"

"I did, but I passed him by. To lose

one arm is enough. I want to keep the other one."

"Which way did he go?" yelled Ahab.

"Let him be. He did you enough harm already."

"Which way!" thundered Ahab.

"Eastward, sir," said the captain softly.

Without another word, Ahab spun around and ordered, "Full speed ahead! Eastward!"

For the next few days, Captain Ahab did not leave the deck except to sleep.

Even his meals were brought to him there. He often climbed the masthead himself to keep watch.

Then on a cold, gray day, the sharp wind whipped across the deck, chilling everyone to the bone. Ahab tapped up and down the deck for a long while. Then he stood still and sniffed at the air like a bloodhound catching a scent.

"He's near. I know it," he said quietly. He peered out over the ocean and suddenly screamed, "There she blows! A hump as white as a snow hill! It is Moby Dick!"

"I see him, too! " shouted Tashtego.

"But I saw him first. The gold piece belongs to me!" said Ahab. "Lower the boats!"

All the boats were dropped. Starbuck

was ordered to stay on the *Pequod* to take care of the ship. Soon oars were ripping through the water towards the whale.

"Keep quiet," whispered Ahab. "We

cannot lose this one. This one is *mine*. Don't scare him away."

The men kept very still, dipping their oars in and out of the water without a sound. As we neared the whale, Ahab hissed softly, "Quiet. Gently. Do not disturb him."

We rowed slower now, careful not to chop the water, which might warn the whale of our approach. The sea was smooth. We carefully glided along until we saw a tremendous white form just under the water's surface.

As it slid by, I was amazed to see that it kept coming and coming. Where was the end? It seemed to be ten times longer than the boat itself! Then it went down deep into the sea, and we could not see it. We waited for what seemed like forever.

Each man was thinking his secret thoughts. Stubb sat there puffing his pipe. Little blue clouds of smoke floated like bubbles from a whale's spout. I looked at Flask. His face was set like stone. Queequeg, Tashtego, and Daggoo were already gripping their harpoons.

Ahab had a strange look. His black eyes glowed like charcoals as he stared down into the sea. Although he was very still, he looked as though he might explode.

These men had spent many years sailing the seas searching for whales. Many times before this, they had waited bravely for the whale to appear. But we all knew that this time it was different. This time it was Moby Dick! It seemed as if he were hunting us! We waited and waited.

Little prickles of hair stood out on the back of my neck. Peering closely at the sea, I saw a white spot. It quickly grew larger and still larger. It was Moby Dick, swimming straight at us! Staying slightly underwater, he skimmed directly under our boat. The whale's back slid along the keel of our boat, barely touching each wooden plank as it went by.

No one said a word. The clouds had cleared, and the sun burned brightly, but I felt a cold sweat wash over my body. Queequeg tightened his big fingers around his harpoon. The muscles in his back strained—ready for the fight.

It was so quiet it seemed the world was standing still. A flock of birds dipped down in flight to circle our boat as though they were watching what would happen. The only sound to be heard was the flapping of their wings as they hovered above us.

A rumble of underwater thunder broke the silence. Suddenly, some distance away, the great white whale smashed through the water's surface. He shot high into the air as though blown from a cannon.

My heart galloped in my chest as I stared at this huge sea monster. Its tremendous, white belly flopped down hard on the water, sending sheets of waves higher than the mainsail of our ship. Then the whale disappeared under the water.

The waves rocked our boat with such great force that we almost overturned. The men were thrown to the back of the boat, piled on top of one another. It took great effort just to hang on to the boat's sides. Our oars flew out of the boat and landed here and there in the churning water, dipping in and out of sight.

Finally, the sea calmed and the boat steadied. We quickly fished the scattered oars out of the sea, glancing around us for a sign of the whale. He was gone. Again we waited.

There it was! The white shadow appeared again. This time he stayed underwater and widely circled the boats. Round and round he swam, creating a swirling ring of waves around us. We were captured in the center of the circle, waiting for the whale to make his move.

Then he stopped. He stayed still for a moment and then lifted his huge head out of the water. His jaws opened wide, showing a long crooked row of sharp teeth. He began heading directly towards Captain Ahab's boat. The harpooners got ready.

Ahab stood up and waited until the great whale was right in front of him.

"Now, Queequeg!" screamed Ahab. "Tashtego! Daggoo!"

The harpooners, using every last bit of their strength, heaved their heavy harpoons into the mouth of the whale. Up, up it went—the most gigantic creature I had ever seen. Sticking out of his mouth like toothpicks, the harpoons did not stop Moby Dick.

Down under the boats he dove. For a moment he was gone. Then we felt our boat shudder. With his mouth opened wide, he came straight up again and sank his teeth into Ahab's boat, taking the boat and everyone in it up into the air.

The men spilled out into the sea, and their oars flew about like sticks of straw. With a thunderous crunch, Moby Dick snapped the boat into two pieces with his jaws. Then he slammed back down into

the water and swam off, his huge fin flapping behind him, swishing great waves of water to each side.

Because of his ivory leg, Captain Ahab could not swim. He grasped the splintered side of a piece of the boat. He was half smothered in foam, yet with his last ounce of strength he shook his fist at the departing whale.

Meanwhile, Starbuck had been watching the battle from the ship. When he first saw the size of Moby Dick he knew *this* was no *ordinary* whale! He brought the *Pequod* to where the drowning men were splashing in the water.

One by one the men were rescued, and with great luck all were alive. With reddened eyes and salt caked in his wrinkles, Ahab was hauled on board. He lay there, half-dead.

Finally, when he could speak, he said, "Help me stand."

"Lay still, sir, and rest awhile," said Starbuck, trying to make Ahab comfortable.

"Help me stand, I say!" demanded Ahab.

Starbuck and Queequeg helped him get up. The men were very quiet, and they stared at their captain as he struggled to stand.

With one hand pointing to his ivory leg and the other pointing out to sea, Ahab screamed, "I will get you, Moby Dick! You have not seen the last of me! I have chased you in my mind through a thousand nightmares. Now that I have finally found you, I will *kill* you."

# Chapter

## 8

# A Battle

Ahab's whaling boat had been smashed. His men were cold, tired, and wet from the day's struggle with the whale. He, himself, had been battered in the fight. In fact, he had come close to being eaten alive by the great white whale. But he refused to rest.

Starbuck and Queequeg offered to clean and bandage his cuts and bruises, but he brushed them away saying, "That whale took my leg. A few more scrapes don't make much difference. I am a tough man, and it is a tough man who will get that whale. It will take Captain Ahab to kill Moby Dick!"

"No more can be done today, sir," said Starbuck, gently. "You can't expect the men to go out again today; all the fight has been knocked out of them. You need rest, supper, and a strong cup of tea. The sun will be setting in a few hours. The whale will still be around tomorrow. We will stay close on his trail. He will not get far. I beg you, sir. Let it go for now."

Ahab was eager to continue the battle, but he knew that he had to wait.

"All right, Starbuck. Tomorrow we fight the whale again. Tell the sailor in the masthead to keep his eyes sharp as an

eagle's. We will follow that whale's course tonight. We will follow that whale to the other side of the world if we must!"

Ahab paced up and down the deck. Every so often he would call up to the sailor on the masthead, "Do you see him?"

Once in a while the sailor would call down, "Yes, sir. Straight ahead." Then Ahab would smile, knowing the *Pequod* was staying on the path of the whale.

Sometimes the sailor would answer, "No, sir. No whale in sight." When this happened, Ahab would command the men to help him climb the masthead to see for himself. He would stay up there until the whale was spotted again.

When a whale sets off in any direction, he usually stays on one straight course. Ahab knew the whale would travel slower at night.

"Down the topsails, Starbuck. We must not run into him until morning."

This done, Ahab settled on deck for the night. Yet every hour he awoke to call out for the whale.

At daybreak the sky began to lighten. First a rosy peach color spread across the east as the sun rose up from the ocean. Then it turned pale blue and slowly deepened in color until the entire sky was a bright, clear blue.

"There she blows!" was heard from above.

The men rushed to the rails where Ahab already stood. They saw the huge

white whale fling its entire body up and out of the ocean.

Stubb, who was standing some distance away from Captain Ahab, said softly, "Oh, you poor beast. You chewed and swallowed the leg of a madman and now he is after you. You had better swim until your lungs burst."

"Catch the wind! Raise the sails!" screamed Ahab. "Get closer to that spout!"

The sails were hoisted high, and the winds blew hard against them. Soon they were blown out as big as a whale's belly as the ship picked up speed. The chase was on!

As the boats were dropped to the water and the men quickly leaped in, Moby Dick turned and swam straight toward the men. Terror struck every man as the foam sprayed a direct path to the boats.

Ahab knew his men needed encouragement. He cheered them on to build up their bravery.

"Only the greatest crew of whalers in the world can catch the great white whale," he shouted to them. "Let me see minds as strong as those iron muscles! Show your guts!"

The whale churned wildly through the water at a furious speed. He looked like a locomotive chugging along with clouds of steam blowing from his spout. He lifted his head from the water. The broad, smooth, white forehead gleamed in the sun. The jaw opened wide, its jagged teeth ready to bite down on anything in its way. His tail lashed powerfully back and forth, pounding waves out to each side. He was so close now, I could see on one side of his

head a large, glassy eye. It was much larger than a man's fist.

"Queequeg! Tashtego! Daggoo! Throw your harpoons!" screamed Ahab.

The spears sailed straight at the whale, stabbing him in the head, in his side, everywhere. The whale did not even blink an eye. As though he had only brushed through a thorny rosebush, he kept coming straight at us.

The oarsmen, showing great skill, steered their boats this way and that and managed to sidestep the huge beast as it shot past us.

Harpoons darted at him from every direction, but this only seemed to make him more angry. He suddenly swam off; he seemed to be gathering up force for a tremendous charge.

Ahab tried to untie some of the tangles in our harpoon lines. That instant, the white whale made a sudden rush at us. He pushed through the snarled lines, dragging Stubb's boat and Flask's boat straight at each other.

The boats hit like clapped hands. The men were thrown into the wild sea below. Pieces of the shattered boats flew in all directions.

The men swirled madly underwater, trying to swim to the surface. Finally reaching air, they grasped at passing pieces of wood from the wrecked boats to try and stay afloat.

Adding to the terror, many sharks had been sighted. The men tried to hoist themselves up onto the wooden planks to escape the deadly sharks.

Flask bobbed up and down like an empty bottle, madly twitching his legs upward onto the oar he had grabbed. Stubb cried out for someone to come and scoop him up from the shark-filled sea. Men everywhere were screaming for help, while the other boats tried to rush to the rescue.

# Chapter

## 9

# Chasing The Whale

Captain Ahab's boat was left unharmed. He quickly began making his way towards the helpless sailors. It was difficult to cross to the men, as the whale had churned the sea into what seemed like a huge kettle of boiling water. His frantic men tried their best to dig through the water, but their efforts were like an eggbeater that scrambled the sea even more.

"Pull together men!" shouted Ahab. "Move the boats! Faster! Faster!"

Just when the boats were beginning to make some progress, Moby Dick appeared. Then a moment later, he shot straight up under Ahab's boat, crashing his huge head into the bottom and lifting it high up in the air.

Clutching the boat's sides, the terrified men stared straight down the cavelike throat of the whale. For one second, the boat hung balanced on the tip of the whale's forehead. Then it toppled over, sending Ahab and his crew into the sea.

Luckily, when Ahab reached the surface, a large piece of his boat was nearby. He grabbed onto the plank of wood and clung tightly to it.

Moments later, Moby Dick swam to the surface. He waited there, a short distance from the wreckage. Whenever a stray board or plank of wood touched him, he flopped his tail to knock it away.

The men stared at the monstrous whale. They kept still, terrified that he would go after a moving target. But soon, as if satisfied that his work for that time was done, he pushed off through the ocean, leaving the men to themselves.

Like the day before, the men on the

*Pequod* were waiting in the distance to come to the aid of the whaling boats. Dropping one of the spare boats, they rescued all the floating seamen. They picked up oars, the bent harpoons, and whatever else could be caught and safely landed on the deck.

It surely was a miracle that all the men had survived, but many were hurt. They lay on deck, groaning in pain from

sprained ankles, shoulders, and wrists. One or two had broken bones where an arm or rib had smashed down on a wooden plank. Some had been hit in the head, and their faces were bruised, purple and swollen. Blood trickled from their wounds, and most of their clothes had been ripped to shreds.

Those of us who had not been hurt took care of the suffering. We made splints for the broken bones and wrapped wounds in clean bandages.

Captain Ahab waited in the water until the last man had been hauled aboard. Then he allowed himself to be pulled up. Every man stared at him as he was helped on board. He leaned heavily on Starbuck. It was then I saw that his ivory leg had been snapped off, leaving just one short splinter.

"You have no broken bones, sir, I hope," said Stubb, coming forward.

"Aye, Stubb. Just one. Broken to bits," he said, pointing to where the ivory leg had been.

"Sir, let me help you to your cabin," said Starbuck to his captain.

"Cabin? No, Starbuck. I will stay right here until we find that whale. There will be no sleep for me until Moby Dick is dead. Then I will sleep a thousand years. Now there is much work to be done. I have a whale to kill!"

He turned his head to the sky and shouted, "You sailor, up there in the masthead, have you seen the whale?"

"Heading eastward, sir," was the answer.

"Raise the sails, men! Down the rest of the spare boats. All able men will serve as crew."

Starbuck stared at Ahab, shocked at his words. "Surely, sir, you cannot be serious."

Ahab looked at Starbuck and the others. He snarled.

"Of course I am serious! The purpose of this voyage is to capture the great white whale. Many years ago, when he bit off my leg with his sharp teeth and swallowed it whole, I swore to come back and kill him. Now, Moby Dick is near! Never again will I have this chance. I must do it now. Nothing will stop me!"

Starbuck was shocked at this outburst. His captain had truly gone mad. His behavior had become more and more strange and now he knew why: Ahab no longer cared about whaling or the sums of money to be made from selling the whale oil. He gave little thought to his family back home who awaited his return. He had seen nearly every port in the world and did not care if he ever saw another. He ate and slept very little, only enough to carry him to the next day so he could

search again for the great white whale. He had only one thing on his mind—Moby Dick.

"Good heavens, sir!" Starbuck began. "Stop this madness! For two days we chased that whale, and a wild beast it is. He nearly killed us all. Must we keep chasing him until the last man is dragged to the bottom of the sea? I beg you, sir, forget this whale. Let us go home."

"Forget this whale?" cried the captain. "This whale that has haunted my dreams, night after night, year after year. This whale that causes me to hobble into my grave. Never! Not until Moby Dick is dead!"

The sky was getting dark. As the sun set in the west, Ahab calmed down. He whispered, "Tomorrow I will kill the great white whale."

# Chapter

10

# Disaster

The sail was shortened as the *Pequod* followed the path of Moby Dick. Again, the sailor in the masthead kept a close watch, peering through his spyglass. He called out to Ahab, "Heading east, sir."

The crew worked late into the night, getting the spare boats ready and sharpening their harpoons, hammering away almost until dawn. The carpenter made Ahab another leg, carved out of a piece of the captain's broken boat.

The nights were dark, and the sea was rocky. But by the morning of the third day, there was calm. A strong breeze in the air picked up the sails and swiftly carried

the *Pequod* across the sea, on our path toward Moby Dick.

Captain Ahab was in an unusually good mood that morning. Standing on deck, leaning on his new leg, he took a deep breath of the salty air and said, "What a lovely day. It is like a summer house for the angels. I have never seen a more beautiful day."

And then, as a cloud crossed the sun, a shadow came over his face. He thought to himself, "If I were the wind, I would blow no more on such a wicked, miserable world."

Looking to the sailor in the masthead he called, "Sailor, what do you see?"

"Nothing, sir," the sailor called down.

"Nothing! And it is almost noon! Lift me up, men. I will find the whale!"

The men once again helped Ahab climb the masthead. An hour passed. The sea was as calm and quiet as a grave. At last, Ahab saw the spout.

"There she blows!" he shouted.

Then to the whale he yelled, "We meet

again, Moby Dick! This will be the last time!"

Ahab made his way down to the deck and looked around to make sure everything was ready. His boat was lowered first. As it started to drop, he saw Starbuck. He reached out for him, and the two men shook hands.

Starbuck had tears in his eyes when he said, "Oh, my captain, my captain! Noble heart—do not go. Do not go!"

Ahab let go of Starbuck's hand and said, "Lower away!"

As the boats pulled off, a swarm of hungry sharks followed close behind, nipping nastily at the oars.

The boats had not gone very far when all around them the water suddenly swelled in big, broad circles. A low, rumbling sound was heard. Everyone held his breath.

Suddenly, the vast bulk of Moby Dick pushed out of the sea, dragging behind a trail of ropes and harpoons. He sprang with such force, that he left a sheet of water against the sky.

"Forward!" shouted Ahab.

Then the boats took off after the whale. But the whale was not running from them; he turned around to face the oncoming boats. He lifted his enormous head out of the water. It looked like a huge marble tombstone. The broad brow was folded in a frown as he came head-on, slapping his tail among the boats.

"*Now*, harpooners!" cried Ahab.

Queequeg shot his spear straight into

the head of the whale as he slid by. Moby Dick flipped his great fin and split the sides of two boats. Water began pouring in through the cracks.

At that moment, a horrible shriek

pierced the air. One of the sailors had been caught in a harpoon rope attached to the whale!

The men stood there, helplessly, as they watched in horror. One last ear split-

ting cry was heard, and then the whale dove down into the water, taking the man with him. No one could do anything for the poor sailor, and now everyone was in danger. I sat by feeling powerless to even help myself.

Ahab watched Moby Dick disappear

deep into the sea with the sailor. Then he looked at his remaining men and their boats. The men in the damaged boats were up to their waists in water.

"Back to the ship!" yelled Ahab to the men in the other boats. "Those boats are destroyed. They will sink soon."

The three boats were swiftly turned and headed back to the ship. The men quickly scampered up the ropes that were lowered for them.

As they looked down, they saw Moby Dick plunge out of the water and head straight towards the ship! Like a huge porcupine with harpoon quills, it charged at a tremendous speed.

His powerful head rammed the side of the ship, making a huge hole in the frame. Then he dove and soon reappeared to make another run at the ship.

Sailors were running about wildly. But there was no where to go to reach safety.

Soon Moby Dick was again at the side of the *Pequod*, making the hole there even

larger. The ship would soon sink, and the sailors would go into the shark-filled sea.

One sailor dashed high up into the masthead, but the ship heaved a mighty groan and then tipped, bow first, into the black water.

Like an arrow shot from a bow, the sailor in the masthead was thrown head-on into the water.

Seeing all this destruction, I buried my head in my arms and cried for that sailor and for all my brave friends.

But Moby Dick was not finished. There was someone still left whom he had to get rid of. It was Captain Ahab.

Diving beneath the sinking ship, the whale ran along the bottom and then came up on the other side. Soon Moby Dick was within a few yards of Ahab's boat.

The sailors trembled. I thought all was surely lost. But the captain stood bravely in the boat, ready to fight the great Moby Dick. He and the whale faced each other—fury and hatred in their eyes.

Ahab grabbed a harpoon and screamed, "It is I who will kill you, Moby Dick! You have taken my leg and my ship and you may take my life, but it will be your final act!"

The whale dove again, but we knew he wasn't running away. We watched and waited for him to reappear. We feared he would come right up under the boat.

Suddenly, not far off, we saw a great burst of water. The whale was heading our way. He lunged forward to attack, baring his long scissor-sharp teeth. He came

straight at Ahab, snorting like a bull on the charge.

Ahab raised his harpoon high into the air and steadied himself in the boat. With all his strength, he pitched the harpoon at the whale.

The harpoon landed straight between Moby Dick's eyes and sank deep into his forehead.

The whale let out an enormous death

groan as it tumbled forward. A fountain of black blood gushed upwards to the sky like an oil well.

It looked as though the fight was over and Captain Ahab had defeated Moby Dick at last. But the whale was not finished.

As Moby Dick spun around, the line of the harpoon caught Ahab around the neck and pulled him out of the boat. It

happened so fast that none of the sailors could get to their feet to help their captain. They were frozen with fear and surprise.

Strangled by his own line, Ahab followed Moby Dick down into the depths of the sea. Nothing was seen of either one again.

Ahab's crew of oarsmen remained frozen with fear and panic. Their eyes bulged at the terrible sight.

For many minutes no one said a word. Everyone kept their eyes on the water's surface. We were all sure Moby Dick would return.

Then we heard another mighty groan. One of the sailors turned around and screamed.

"Look! The ship!" he yelled.

The ship was sinking into the sea. Huddling close together, the men were not sure of what to do. We all sat there staring in wonder as the *Pequod* made its dive. It seemed to be following its captain to his lonely ocean grave.

As the ship sank and the sailors on board fell into the sea, all the men in the whaling boat looked around at one another. We all realized that Moby Dick was not returning. But we were not out of danger. We were adrift at sea, with little hope of being rescued. What after all were our chances of seeing a ship pass by? And, would a ship even see us?

We all began to think that the worst would happen—that we, too, would soon join Ahab, Moby Dick, and the *Pequod* below the surface of the black sea. No one spoke it, but the fear in the men's eyes said it all.

We watched the ship sink, and with it we felt all hope disappear.

# Chapter

11

# The Rescue

The bow of the *Pequod* had disappeared into the dark water and the stern was completely out of the sea, high up in the air. Men were being thrown off at every moment. As the boat kept tilting forward, the men lost their balance and slid straight into the sea.

The wide white sails fluttered and sagged like a huge dying ghost.

As the boat sank lower, the sharks circled, snapping at the drowning men.

I raised my head to the sky and thought of my home, as the stinging tears blinded my eyes. Would I never again see the familiar faces of my family and friends? I longed to run along the sloping green hills. I wanted so badly to be safe and secure, away from all this madness and violence.

All at once, my boat shook. It gave a lurch forward and down it went. As I hit the water, I let go and started swimming as fast as I could.

With long reaching strokes, I pulled myself through and up and over the rolling waves. After going some distance, I saw a wooden coffin that had been stored aboard the *Pequod*, and I grabbed onto it.

As I floated away on the coffin, I looked back to where the *Pequod* had been. The great force of the ship plunging down, down to the bottom of the sea made a huge whirlpool.

The whirling mass of water spun around and around, sucking everything into it. Men, boats, oil barrels, harpoons— everything in reach was dragged into the swirling tunnel of the sea.

The last thing I saw was the flag that flew high over the *Pequod*. It waved once

more above the water. Then down it went, down for good.

Little by little the waves' fury was broken, and the sea began to calm. To my great relief, the sharks that had been following me swam away.

I drifted for days lying flat on the top of the coffin. The hot sun burned my skin, and I was nearly crazy with thirst. Soon, I could not think clearly.

By the time the sun went down each

night, my arms and legs were numb from the chill of the water. I was so cold, that through the long nights my bones rattled against the coffin. Worse still, I was alone.

I awoke each morning hoping to see a ship coming to rescue me. At first, I thought that surely my luck had not run out. But soon I lost all hope. Without food or water, I knew that I could not last much longer. Then when the sharks began to circle my coffin, I knew that soon I would leave this world and end up in an ocean grave.

Happily, one morning I awoke to the sound of a human voice, instead of the usual lapping of water against the coffin.

"Ahoy, there!" it said.

I blinked my eyes and pinched my skin. Was it a dream? Was it true?

I looked hard toward the horizon. I thought I could see a great ship in the distance and a small boat coming my way. But maybe I was losing my mind.

"Ahoy there, mate. Grab this rope!"

It was not my imagination. A passing

ship had spotted me and had sent a boat to rescue me! The sailors were now right by my coffin, throwing me a line.

I was half-dead from exhaustion when the men dragged me into their boat.

I had no strength to help them pull me in. I only looked back to watch my coffin float away with the passing waves.

"Water," I whispered.

My throat was almost swollen shut

from thirst. The cool sips they gave me dripped down my burning throat. I could not believe my good fortune.

However, I began to think of Captain Ahab and Moby Dick. Suddenly, I was trembling with the thought of staying out on the dangerous sea.

"Where are we going?" I asked, in a choked voice.

"Home, lad. We are all going home."

THE END

# ABOUT THE AUTHOR

HERMAN MELVILLE was born on August 1, 1819 in New York City. When he was only twelve years old, his father died. Because his family was left penniless, young Melville had to go to work. Melville's first jobs included working as a clerk in a bank, as a cabin boy on a ship traveling to England, and as a teacher in an elementary school.

In January 1841, he joined a whaling ship called the *Acushnet*. He sailed throughout the Pacific Ocean, then returned to the United States to tell of his adventures. Soon, he began writing stories based on his experience at sea. In 1850, Melville got married and settled in Massachusetts, where he started writing *Moby Dick*.

Melville was a well-known writer for a while. But when he died, on September 28, 1891, most people had forgotten his name. Now Melville is regarded as one of America's greatest writers. And *Moby Dick* is considered one of America's greatest works.

# The Young Collector's
# Illustrated Classics

Adventures of Robin Hood
Black Beauty
Call of the Wild
Dracula
Frankenstein
Heidi
Little Women
Moby Dick
Oliver Twist
Peter Pan
The Prince and the Pauper
The Secret Garden
Swiss Family Robinson
Treasure Island
20,000 Leagues Under the Sea
White Fang